DISCARDED

Saving Grace

Darlene Ryan

orca soundings

D0187850

Orca Book Publishers

Library and Archives Canada Cataloguing in Publication

Ryan, Darlene, 1958-

Saving Grace / written by Darlene Ryan.

(Orca Soundings)
ISBN 10: 1-55143-668-X (bound).--ISBN 10: 1-55143-508-X (pbk.)
ISBN 13: 978-1-55143-668-5 (bound).--ISBN 13: 978-1-55143-508-4 (pbk.)

I. Title. II Series.

PS8635.Y35S29 2006   jC813'.6   C2006-903257-2

Summary: Evie is determined to care for her baby—even if it means
kidnapping her.

First published in the United States, 2006
Library of Congress Control Number: 2006928468

Orca Book Publishers gratefully acknowledges the support for its publishing
programs provided by the following agencies: the Government of Canada
through the Book Publishing Industry Development Program and the
Canada Council for the Arts, and the Province of British Columbia
through the BC Arts Council and the Book Publishing Tax Credit.

Cover design by Lynn O'Rourke
Cover photography by Getty Images

Orca Book Publishers
PO Box 5626 Station B
Victoria, BC Canada
V8R 6S4

Orca Book Publishers
PO Box 468
Custer, WA USA
98240-0468

www.orcabook.com
Printed and bound in Canada.
Printed on 100% PCW recycled paper.
11 10 09 08 • 5 4 3 2

For Judy

Chapter One

I ran across the bare front yard. What kind of home for a kid didn't even have any grass? I shoved the car seat onto the front seat of the truck and jumped in.

"Go!" I yelled at Justin.

He stared at me with his mouth hanging open. "Jesus, Evie," he said. "What the hell did you do?"

"Will you just drive? Come on. Move the damn truck. Go!"

"Go where?"

I leaned across the baby seat and smacked his arm. "I don't care. Just get us out of here now."

Finally Justin put the truck in gear and pulled away from the curb. I frigged with the seat belt, trying to thread it through the bottom part of the car seat. The baby was still asleep.

I got the belt buckled, sat back and fastened my own. We got to the stop sign where the road from the subdivision crossed the old highway. "That way," I said, pointing to the right.

Justin looked over at me. Then he looked at the baby. But he turned and started up the old river road. "You said you just wanted to see her," he said.

"So I lied."

"Evie, you can't just take someone else's kid."

I reached into the car seat and stroked the baby's cheek with one finger. It was the softest thing I had ever felt. Bits of dark hair, the same color as mine, stuck out from under her pink hat. "I didn't steal someone else's kid, Justin," I said. "She's mine and I'm keeping her."

Justin pulled one hand back through his own hair. "Dammit," he muttered.

Okay, so he was kind of pissed. But he'd change his mind. He'd see that this was the right thing to do. And anyway, I knew how to get around Justin.

I looked down at the baby again. My baby. Not the Hansens'. They weren't even good parents. I knew because I'd been watching that house for almost two weeks. They left her with a babysitter all day. Okay, so she was Mr. Hansen's mother, but still. They wanted a baby so much, that's what they'd said on their profile, but then they didn't even spend any time with her. And there weren't any other little babies around there for her to play with when she got bigger, just a big empty lot on one side of that place and a house that had been abandoned, half built, on the other.

That half-finished house turned out to be good for me because I could watch my baby from there but no one could see me. It wasn't really like I was trying to hide. I just hadn't figured out what I was going to do and I didn't want people bugging me.

At first the only thing I'd wanted to do was see my baby, you know, make sure she was okay. I'd only gotten to see her once after she was born because my dad said it would be easier that way. When we got home from the hospital he'd said, "It's done now. Put it out of your head." It was like he didn't realize I had just given up my own flesh and blood. I didn't even say anything. I just walked away and went to my room and shut the door. My insides hurt, ached, and I thought that was just from having her, from pushing and all, but that feeling never went away. I couldn't just "put it out of my head." Finally I knew I had to see for myself that my baby was all right.

My dad had put all the adoption papers in that metal box he kept in the back of his closet. And I knew where he hid the key—in his sock drawer. Once I knew the Hansens' full names it was easy to go online at the library and find their address. So the next morning I cut school and hitched out there. I took a clipboard. I was going to go to the door and pretend I was doing a survey, but then when I saw the empty house next door, with no one working in it, I figured why not just watch for a while.

My mom liked to go bird-watching. She had a great big book all about birds, and she used to let me look at the pictures. After she died, Dad put all her stuff in boxes in the basement. I had to go through five boxes to find her binoculars. I figured she wouldn't mind me using them to check on her granddaughter.

And that's all I was going to do—just watch my baby. But the more I watched, the more I could see she needed me. In the end I knew I had to do something because a baby needs to be with her mother. And it was easy, which just proves they weren't good parents, because instead of me it could have been some weirdo who walked away with her.

Every time Mr. Hansen's mother came back from somewhere, she'd put the baby in her car seat on the deck while she carried stuff in—groceries and dry-cleaning and stuff. What kind of a grandmother was she, leaving the baby out there like that? My mom would never have done that with her granddaughter.

All I had to do was wait by the corner of the house. I did lie to Justin. I told him I just wanted to look in a window and see her. It was easier than getting into a long explanation beforehand. I knew once he'd spent some time with his daughter he'd see that the three of us were meant to be a family.

Chapter Two

I glanced at Justin. He must have felt me looking at him. "I thought this was all decided," he said. He didn't take his eyes off the road.

"I never decided anything," I said. "My father did. He said, 'Just because you were stupid enough to get yourself pregnant doesn't mean you're going to ruin the rest of your life.' He's the one who called the social worker. He's the one who went through all the files on the people she picked out. He decided on the Hansens. Not me."

Justin shrugged. "I thought they seemed nice."

"Yeah, well they're not Brianna's real parents. She should be with her real mother. Me."

"Brianna? I thought her name was Grace or something like that."

"Her name is Brianna now. Grace is an old-lady name."

"So now what?" Justin said. "Do you have some kind of plan or are we just going to drive around forever?"

I didn't like the snarky sound in his voice.

"Of course I have a plan," I said. "You think I'm stupid? We're going to Montreal. Why do you think I told you to turn right back there?"

"I'm not driving all the way to Montreal," Justin said.

"Well, we can't exactly stay around here, can we?" I said. Sometimes he was so stunned.

"Yeah, but why Montreal?"

"Because it's a big place. No one will find us there."

"All you told me was you wanted to see her. You didn't say anything about taking her, about going to Montreal."

I reached over and squeezed his leg. "I'm sorry, okay? I just didn't know if you'd help me if I told you what I was going to do."

"I wouldn't have."

"See? That's why I didn't tell you."

Justin made a growling sound in the back of his throat. He reached for the radio. I grabbed his hand. "No, you can't put that on," I said. "You'll wake the baby."

Justin yanked his hand away and held it up between us. "Don't talk to me, Evie," he said.

That was fine with me. We drove in silence for a while, just the headlights of the truck shining through the darkness. Then I heard a whimper from the car seat. The baby's little face was twisted into a frown and she was waving her arms, her two tiny hands clenched into fists. I leaned over to tuck the blanket around her a bit better, but she started crying. For a little baby she was loud.

The truck zigzagged on the road. "Christ, Evie," Justin said. "Do something. I almost went in the ditch."

"She's just hungry," I said. I reached for my backpack on the floor. I'd brought everything I figured Brianna would need—bottles, diapers, blankets. I gave the bottle of formula a shake and took the cap off. "Here, sweetie," I said, putting the nipple in her mouth. She sucked on it for a minute, then made a sour face and spit the nipple back out again, crying even louder than before.

"Why doesn't she want it?" Justin said.

"I don't know," I snapped. "Maybe she's not hungry. Maybe her diaper's wet or something." I slid my hand partway under Brianna's backside. Her sleeper thingy didn't feel wet, and the diaper didn't seem very squishy. I stuck the bottle in her open mouth again. She barely drank any before she spit it out, and she turned her face away when I tried again. And she kept on doing that. She'd take maybe one drink and then spit out the nipple and cry again. Over and over.

Chapter Three

"Justin, you have to pull over," I said finally. He didn't hear me. I leaned across the seat and whacked his arm with the back of my hand. "Pull over," I said again.

"What for?"

"I wanna burp her."

"So? Do it."

"I have to take her out of the seat, asshole," I said, shouting so he'd hear me over Brianna's crying. "Just pull over."

Justin puffed out his cheeks and then let out a breath. "Fine," he grumbled through clenched teeth. He slowed down, pulled over onto the gravel side of the road and put the truck in park. Then he turned off the ignition, grabbed the keys and got out. I heard him swearing under his breath.

Brianna was still hollering. Her face was all red and wrinkly and her eyes were squeezed shut. Geez, how could someone so small make so much noise? The sound made my stomach into a big, hard knot.

I lifted her out of the seat. She was heavier than I'd thought and hard to hold with her arms and legs going all over the place. She hadn't taken very much of the bottle, but I knew she had to be burped anyway.

When I'd decided that Brianna needed to be with me, I'd gone to the library and gotten the biggest book on babies I could find. And I'd read it from one end to the other. I had taken a babysitting class at the Y, but that was three years ago. And I hadn't paid attention to everything. It had been my dad's idea for me to go in the first place, so I could earn my own money instead of him always having to give me an allowance.

"Shush, shush," I said. I held Brianna up against my shoulder the way they'd showed us in the class. Between what I remembered and the book, I knew a lot about babies. I rubbed Brianna's back as she twisted and squirmed, but she wouldn't burp. She coughed a couple of times. She even tried to climb up over my shoulder. Mostly she cried. And I wanted to cry too. "Please burp," I whispered against her ear.

I could hear Justin pacing behind the truck. After a couple of minutes he came and opened the driver's door. "Can't you get her to stop?" he asked.

"Shut up," I said.

Justin looked out the windshield and then back at me. "This was a mistake, Evie. We have to go back."

"No!" My heart started beating so hard it seemed like I could hear it. "I'm not going back." I wrapped both arms tightly around Brianna. "I'm not giving her up again. I won't do it." The baby started hollering even louder.

"Geez, you're going to squish her," Justin said. "You're holding her too tight. Even I know that."

I loosened my grip a little. "The only place I'm going is Montreal. Nobody is taking my baby from me." I stared hard at him so he'd know how serious I was.

"Christ!" he said finally. He slammed the door and walked away again. I could hear him kicking gravel at the back tires.

I set Brianna back in the car seat. I had little packages of baby cereal, plain or with banana. Maybe she'd eat that. It was the organic kind, so it had to be good for her.

I found the little baby spoon and the bowl with dancing bears on it I'd bought at Wal-Mart and opened the box of banana-flavored cereal. It smelled pretty good.

Mixed up with water, the stuff reminded me of that goopy paste we'd used in art class in about grade five. I offered Brianna a tiny spoonful. She turned her head from one side to the other, trying to get away from the spoon.

"C'mon, sweetie, try it, please." I pressed the spoon against her mouth—not too hard. She made a face and swatted at it with one hand.

Justin opened the truck door again and leaned against the seat. I couldn't get Brianna to open her mouth. Then I remembered something my mom used to do when she looked after the kids down our street. I held the spoon up in the air. "Here comes the airplane, flying home to the airport," I said. I made the spoon do loops in the air. "Ready for landing. Open hangar doors." It didn't work. Brianna's lips stayed pressed together. "Oh c'mon, Brianna," I said.

Just then Justin leaned over, swiped his finger through the bowl and stuck it in his mouth. He made a face. Then he turned and spit on the ground. "That's crap!" he said, wiping spit off the side of his mouth with his hand. "I don't blame her. I wouldn't eat that crud either."

I reached over and slapped the side of his head. "You are so stupid," I yelled. "You put your dirty fingers in her food."

"Geez, relax, it was just one finger," Justin said, holding it up. "Don't get all freaky. It's not like I spit in the dish or something."

"Well, I can't feed her any of that now. It's all full of germs."

"In case you hadn't noticed, she wasn't eating anything."

"You're such a pig," I said. "It's... it's...all contaminated."

"Great. I guess we won't be needing this anymore then," Justin said. He grabbed the bowl and whipped it like a Frisbee across the ditch and into the bushes. "We're going home," he yelled. "You're giving that baby back. This is a freakin' disaster."

I couldn't help it. My eyes filled with tears and some of them spilled over and slipped down my face. I tried to wipe them away but they kept on coming. There was a lump in my throat I couldn't seem to swallow away.

I put one arm across the front of the car seat. "Please, Justin, please," I begged. "I love her. I can't give her to someone else. I'm her family. We're her family. Not them." My nose was running. I wiped it on the edge of my sleeve. "Please. I can't go back." I took a couple of jerky breaths.

Justin's eyes were angry and his teeth were clenched. He turned away, slammed the door and then kicked the truck a couple of times. I heard him walk away. Then there was nothing but silence.

Chapter Four

Brianna had stopped crying. She'd fallen asleep again. Her head was kind of slumped forward. Her nose was running too. I found a Kleenex in my pocket and carefully wiped her nose first, then my own. She didn't wake up. I wiped my face with the edge of my sweater because I didn't want to waste any more Kleenex.

I started putting the rest of my stuff in my bag. I'd meant what I'd said to Justin. I wasn't going back. I couldn't. I opened the truck door on my side and climbed out so I could check around on the floor to make sure I had everything.

Justin grabbed my shoulder from behind. I sucked in a breath and almost fell onto the dirt. "What the hell are you doing, Evie?" he said.

"Let go of me!" I gave him a shove. He stumbled back but kept his balance.

"What are you doing?" he said again.

I glanced inside the truck. Brianna was still asleep. I turned to face Justin. "I'm not going back," I said, hands jammed in my pockets. "You want to go back? Go ahead. Brianna and I will be fine without you." My mouth was suddenly so dry my lips were sticking to my teeth. "I'm going to Montreal, Justin. I'm not going home and I'm not giving up my baby."

"How're you getting to Montreal?" Justin asked.

"I'll hitch."

"With a kid? Yeah, sure. There's a good idea." He made a face and rolled his eyes.

"Okay, so I have some money. We'll take the bus."

"You don't even know where there's a bus stop or what time the next bus is," Justin said.

"Well, it's not your problem, is it, Justin?" I said softly.

He gritted his teeth and closed his eyes for a second. "Get in the truck, Evie," he said at last, not looking at me.

I turned away from him and felt around on the floor. My water bottle had rolled partway underneath the seat. I stuffed the bottle in the side pocket of the backpack.

"Stop," Justin said, grabbing my arm. "I'm not going to just leave you here." He let out a breath. "I'll drive you, okay? I'm sorry. Just get in the truck before she starts crying again."

I didn't say anything or even look at him, but I climbed onto the seat and fastened my belt.

We drove for I don't know how long without talking. I didn't want to talk anyway. All I wanted to do was look at Brianna. I leaned my head back against the seat and touched her tiny fist. She grabbed my finger. Her own little fingers were so strong. I smiled. My baby was strong. She coughed a couple of times and made a face but went on sleeping. I closed my eyes and thought about the wonderful life the three of us were going to have in Montreal.

I woke up with a kink in my neck. And my left foot was asleep. I hadn't meant to doze off. I peeked at Brianna. She was still asleep, and there was a tiny spit bubble between her lips. I sat up a little straighter and stretched. "How long was I asleep," I asked Justin.

"I don't know. An hour or so," he said. "You snore."

"I do not."

He grinned. "Yeah, you do."

I stuck my tongue out at him. Even though Justin and I had done it a lot, we'd never *slept* together—I mean in the same bed, all night. There was a lot of stuff I didn't know about him, or him about me. It didn't matter though. There was lots of time for all that once we got to Montreal.

"What are you gonna do for money when you get to Montreal?" Justin asked after a while.

"I have some money," I said.

"How much?"

"Enough until I get a job." Actually I had a lot of money. My mom used to put money in a bank account in my name every month—"for your education," she'd say. The bankbook had been in my dad's box in the closet with the adoption papers. I'd gone to the bank and taken all the money out of the account. Brianna was more important than my education. My mom would have understood that.

Justin shot me a quick look. "You're fifteen and you don't speak French. What kind of a job can you get?"

"They speak English in Montreal too," I snapped. "And for your information I'm going to get a job working for a fashion designer."

Justin gave a snort of laughter. "What do you know about fashion?" he said. "You can't even sew. You cut off the bottom of your jeans and left them all ragged. You put tape on the bottom of your skirt."

"I didn't say I was going to make clothes, you dink. I said I want to design them. You know, draw. Eventually. I have to work my way up. Ms. Carrington said I have a lot of artistic talent."

Justin laughed. "Yeah, like Gorilla Legs would know."

"Shut up," I yelled. I reached over to smack him and bumped the car seat. Brianna started to cry. "See what you did?" I said.

"Shush, shush," I crooned to the baby, stroking her head. "Mama's here." She wouldn't stop. The twisted lump in my stomach came back.

"Can't you shut her up?" Justin said.

"She's a baby," I said. "They cry, asshole." I felt around in my pack and found the bottle of formula. Brianna didn't like it any better this time than she had before. I couldn't get her to take even one drink. She just kept spitting the nipple right back out again as fast as I got it in her mouth. And it wasn't easy getting it in her mouth in the first place. My ears were ringing from her crying. I knew she had to be hungry, so why wouldn't she eat? Were kids picky eaters even when they were this little?

Chapter Five

I caught sight of the water bottle stuck in the side pocket of my bag. I grabbed it, unscrewed the cap and carefully dribbled a bit of water into Brianna's mouth. She sputtered and coughed and some of the water ran onto her chin, but she swallowed and then she turned to me and opened and closed her mouth like a baby bird. I got out an empty baby bottle and filled it a bit more than halfway with water. This time, when I stuck the nipple in Brianna's mouth, she drank.

The knot in my stomach let go. "See?" I said to Justin. "It's not like you have to go to school or something to be a mother. When it's your own baby it's natural. It just happens."

"Yeah, whatever," he muttered.

Brianna drank the whole bottle of water. "You have to pull over," I told Justin when she was done.

"Again?" he grumbled. "How're we supposed to get to Montreal if I keep having to stop all the time?"

"I have to burp her, so I have to take her out of the car seat. I can't do that when you're driving because it's not safe. Just pull over already, okay?"

Justin shook his head, but he pulled onto the shoulder of the road and put the truck in park. He looked at me. "Well, c'mon. Get on with it."

I took Brianna out of the seat and put her up on my shoulder again. She fussed and squirmed as I tried to rub her back.

"You know, she's just like you, Evie," Justin said, watching us. "She can't stay still for even a minute."

I gave Brianna's back a couple of gentle pats and she made a small *urp* sound. "Yeah, well she's nothing like you, Justin," I said. "When you burp you sound like a pig."

The baby lifted her head and looked at me. Her nose was running again. "Get me a Kleenex, Justin," I said. "They're in the bottom of the bag somewhere."

He leaned over and felt around in the backpack. "I can't find them," he said after a minute or so. "Here." He grabbed a paper napkin from Dairy Queen off the dusty dash. "Use this."

"I'm not using that," I said. "For one thing, it's filthy, and for another, it's too rough for her nose." I held Brianna out to him. "Hold her for a second and I'll find a Kleenex."

Justin held up both hands. "No way, I'm not holding her."

"She won't bite or anything. Take her."

"No." Justin grabbed the backpack and started shoving things around inside. "Here," he said after a few seconds, pulling out a Kleenex. "Blow her nose and then put her back in the seat. We need to get going."

I wiped Brianna's nose. She didn't like that either. She tried to turn her head away, and she scrunched up her face and made a couple of funny grunting noises. That made me laugh because that grunting noise was the same kind of sound Justin made when he drank beer. She was like him after all.

I got her fastened back in the car seat with a new blanket because we'd gotten some water on the old one. She put the end of one fist in her mouth and chewed on it while she watched me. I offered her a finger and she grabbed onto it with her other hand. Justin pulled back onto the road. In a few minutes Brianna's eyelids began to droop. Pretty soon she was asleep again.

Chapter Six

There wasn't much traffic on the road. Once in a while a car went by us going in the other direction. I lay my head back against the seat and closed my eyes for just a second. I didn't really mean to fall asleep again, but I did.

I dreamed about my mother. In the dream she wasn't dead. I'd come home and she was in the kitchen making a devil's food chocolate cake—my all-time favorite. I just stood there in the doorway staring at her. Finally she turned around and smiled at me. "Hi," she said. "How was your day?" She had flour on the front of her jeans.

"You're dead," I said.

Mom laughed. "No I'm not. See? I'm right here." She looked just the way she had the very last time I'd seen her—I mean the last time I'd seen her when she was alive. She was wearing jeans and a red shirt with her hair piled up on her head.

"No! I know you're dead," I said. "There was an accident. A truck came across the road and...and hit your car. I... we had a funeral. I saw you in the..."

Mom shrugged. "Wasn't me." She gestured at the counter. "You want to lick the bowl?" she asked.

"I can't believe it," I said. "I missed you so much every day. I'm so glad you're here." I rushed across the room and threw my arms around her, but it was like she was made of air. She just faded away into nothing. I grabbed for her but there was nothing to hold on to.

I woke up with a start. It didn't matter how many times I dreamed about my mom. She was still dead when I woke up.

I straightened up and stretched. My head had been slumped over against the car seat, and my mouth was all sticky inside. I felt around on the truck floor, found the water bottle and drank what was left. It wasn't very cold anymore.

"Where are we?" I asked Justin. My ponytail had come half undone. I pulled the elastic loose and raked my fingers through the knots in my hair.

"We're getting pretty close to Edmundston," he said.

"How long before we get to Montreal?"

"Hours."

"You know, we'd make better time on the highway," I said.

"Yeah," he said. "Except the cops are probably looking for you by now. We have to stay off the main roads. You did kidnap a baby, you know, Evie."

"Don't say that," I said, twisting my hair back into a ponytail again. "She's mine. You can't kidnap your own kid."

Justin had turned the radio on low while I'd been asleep. "Hey, that's our song," I said.

"What do you mean, 'our song'?" Justin said.

I turned the sound up just a notch and sang along, keeping my voice low so Brianna wouldn't wake up. "...when you touch me, I can hardly breathe, when you touch me, I still believe." I looked at Justin. "I can't believe you don't remember. That's the first song we danced to, the very first time we made love."

He shrugged. "Whatever."

"Justin! That's the night we met. How can you not remember?"

"I remember meeting you. I just don't remember dancing and songs and stuff like that."

How could he have forgotten? I'd told my dad that I was sleeping over at Jade's that night. She'd been my best friend

since grade two, except now her mom
didn't want Jade hanging around with me
anymore because I got pregnant. Jade's
mother said I was a bad influence. But
back then we hung out all the time. I'd
say I was staying at Jade's, and she'd
tell her mother she was sleeping over
at my place. That way we could go out
and no one would ask where we were
going and when we would be home. That
had always worked because no one ever
checked, and most of the time when one
of us said we were sleeping over at the
other's house we really were.

That night we'd gone to a party Evan
Kelly was having out at his parents'
camp. Most of the kids at the party were
in high school, but Jade had been invited
by this guy, Dylan, who she'd met at the
Y pool, and he'd said she could bring a
friend. And that was me.

So anyway, Dylan had grabbed Jade as
soon as we got there. Someone gave me a
beer and I just wandered around at first.
I didn't really like beer—I'd sneaked a

few sips of my dad's and the taste was gross—but I couldn't say no because I didn't want it to look like I wasn't cool.

I didn't really know anybody, and Jade was already in Dylan's lap, so after a while I went outside on the deck because it was just too loud inside. There were steps that went all the way down to the beach, and Justin was sitting on the top one smoking a cigarette.

I didn't usually go for guys who smoked because when they stuck their tongue in your mouth it tasted really raunchy. Plus I hated the smell in my hair. I've always spent a lot of effort on my hair, and I never bought cheap shampoo or conditioner, and I didn't want to smell like some old, stinky cigarette when I was spending fifteen bucks a bottle for conditioner. But Justin was blowing these totally cool smoke rings, perfect circles that just floated away into the dark.

I didn't know who he was then. I mean, I'd seen him around the Y pool and at the Burger Barn and the mall, and I'd noticed him because how could you not? But I didn't even know his name then. He was so cute, tall with strong arms, and he had his hair long then too, thick and blond and almost touching his shoulders. So I just watched him for a while and didn't say anything. Then he turned around and smiled at me, and it was just like in the movies—for a second I couldn't breathe.

He put out his cigarette on the end of the railing and then he pulled a pack of gum out of his pocket and offered me a piece.

"Thanks," I said. I leaned against the railing, peeled off the paper wrapper, popped the gum in my mouth—it was spearmint—and hoped I didn't look too much like a cow when I was chewing.

Justin slid over on the stairs. "Have a seat," he said.

I sat down next to him. The step was so narrow our legs touched. I hoped he couldn't feel mine shaking.

"I'm Justin," he said.

"I'm Evie."

"You here with anyone?"

I knew he meant a guy. I shook my head. "Just my friend Jade. She's inside."

"I've seen you around," Justin said. "At the pool, right?"

I nodded. "Uh-huh." He'd noticed me. We just started talking then. About how it wasn't fair that now you had to buy a punch pass to swim at the Y instead of just paying three bucks every time. And how the parking lot at the Dairy Queen up the hill was getting too crazy to hang out in.

We talked for maybe an hour. It was getting cold, and Justin took off his sweatshirt and gave it to me to wear. It was so romantic. A while later we went inside to find something to eat. After, Justin said, "You wanna dance?" and we did. That's how "When You Touch Me" got to be our song because it was playing on the radio.

I had my head on Justin's shoulder and I could smell his aftershave and I thought, I could die right now and I'd be happy. Then later we went for a walk down the beach and found this spot beside a big rock, kind of back in the bushes. We sat on the blanket that Justin had brought and we started kissing, and soon Justin had his hand on my bare back. He was whispering in my ear how much he wanted me, and my insides were melting.

I didn't just put out like that, though, especially for someone I'd just met, but with Justin I knew it was different. We were already falling in love, you know, like love at first sight. I pulled back for a second. "We don't have any...you know, protection," I said.

"I sort of do," Justin said.

"What do you mean, sort of?" I asked.

"My buddy, Cameron, him and his girlfriend, they're in love and everything. I think they'll probably even get married some day, but his parents are really religious and strict and all, and so he asked me to hold onto his—you know—protection, because if they found it they'd freak." He ran his finger down my cheek and across my lips. "I've never done anything like this before," he said. "And if you don't want to..."

I thought my heart was going to burst right out of my chest, it was pounding so hard. "I want to," I said.

Chapter Seven

After that night, Justin and I were together all the time. We had to kind of keep things secret. I was fourteen and he was nearly seventeen. My dad would have gone ballistic. I couldn't even tell Jade, which I hated because she was my best friend and I wouldn't have even been at the party and met Justin if it hadn't been for her. Justin said that as soon as I turned sixteen we could tell everyone, but then the condom broke.

We were in Justin's truck back in the woods off the road to the landfill. He sat up and I heard him say, "Oh crap."

"What is it?" I said, pulling on my underpants and jeans.

"It broke."

"What broke? What do you mean?"

"The condom. It broke."

"I thought they weren't supposed to break."

"Yeah, well this one did." Justin hauled up his pants and fastened his belt.

I counted back in my head. "It's probably okay," I said. "My period's gonna start in about a week."

Justin was pulling his hand back through his hair the way he always did when something was bugging him. "Isn't there some kind of pill you can get from the doctor?" he said. "That can keep you from getting pregnant?"

"I don't know," I said. "Anyway, I can't go to the doctor. The first thing he'll do is call my dad." I put my arms around Justin's neck. "I'm sure it'll be okay. I'm really, really regular. You'll see."

And my period started right on time on the fourteenth, though it only lasted a couple of days. Justin and I were super careful after that, but the next month I missed my period altogether, and then a couple of weeks after I should have gotten it, I thought I had the flu. I got up and puked even before I'd washed my hair. It happened the next morning too. The third morning my dad said he was taking me to the clinic because I couldn't keep missing school.

The doctor was a woman. Dr. Marriot. She was filling in because Dr. Tracey was away. She had on a long floaty skirt and flat sandals with her white doctor coat, and she reminded me of Ms. Carrington, my art teacher. Except Ms. Carrington usually wore her sandals with socks. The doctor had blue polish on her toes and a silver toe ring.

I sat up on the table in the examining room while she looked down my throat, felt my neck and listened to me breathe. I told her how I'd heaved, first thing, for the past three mornings. "Are you sexually active, Evie?" she asked.

I wasn't sure whether I should tell her. I didn't want my dad to find out and get Justin into trouble. If it had been Dr. Tracey, I wouldn't have said a word.

"Anything you say to me stays in this room," she said when I didn't answer.

I let out a breath I hadn't realized I was holding and nodded. She gave me a little bottle and sent me into the bathroom to pee.

"It has to be a mistake," I said when she told me I was pregnant. "Because we've been super, super careful. Okay, there was that one time last month, but— I mean, I got my period so how could I be pregnant?"

"Was it a normal period?" she asked.

"Well, it was kind of light and it only lasted a couple of days."

The doctor explained that what I'd thought was just a short period really hadn't been one at all.

"Would you like me to tell your father?" she said.

I nodded. I could have puked right then, but there was nothing left in my stomach.

Dad didn't scream at me, which I'd known he wouldn't do with someone else around, but his face got so red I thought for a second the top of his head would blow off. "How could you have been so goddamn stupid, Evie?" he said finally in a quiet voice. He kept squeezing his hands into fists and then letting go again.

I didn't say anything. What could I say?

The doctor started talking about vitamins and nutrition and stuff like that. "What about an abortion?" my father interrupted.

"It's an option," Dr. Marriot said. "There'd have to be another doctor in agreement."

"No," I shouted. "I'm having my baby."

"You're just a kid yourself," Dad said. "How the hell can you raise a baby? No. You're not going to ruin your life over this."

"I don't care," I said. "If you try to make me have an abortion I'll run away." My hands were clenched so tightly I could feel my fingernails cutting into my hands.

Dr. Marriot put her hand on my arm. "Let's all take a deep breath," she said. My father and I glared at each other. I could feel the anger in the air—the same prickliness there is right before a thunderstorm.

"It's a big decision," Dr. Marriot said. "Why don't you go home? Take a few days. Think about everything. Then come back and see me and we'll talk about the options."

Dad and I got in the car and headed home without talking. He wouldn't look at me either. When we pulled into the driveway, he turned off the engine and just sat there. Finally he let out a long breath. "Who's the father, Evie?" he asked.

"You don't know him," I said. "And I'm not having an abortion. I mean it. I really will run away."

"Then you'll put the baby up for adoption," he said. "There's no way I'm letting you throw away your life over something like this."

We went inside the house and I went up to my room. I stood sideways in front of my mirror and lifted my shirt. You couldn't tell there was a baby growing inside me. I lay my hand on my stomach. I couldn't feel anything. It didn't even feel real, but my and Justin's baby was inside me.

Chapter Eight

Of course I had to tell my dad who the baby's father was. Dad went to see Justin's parents. I don't know what happened, but they all decided it was better for everyone if they just gave my dad some money and Justin and I didn't see each other anymore.

But we still managed to be together. I figured, why shouldn't I be with Justin?

I mean, we loved each other, and it wasn't like anything was going to happen because it already had. It wasn't easy, because Dad was watching me all the time, plus Jade's mother wouldn't let her hang around me anymore so she wasn't any help. Jade was kinda pissed at me anyway because I hadn't told her about Justin in the first place.

I got out of last class a couple of times by signing my dad's name on a note saying I had a doctor's appointment. Then Justin picked me up just down the street from the school. And I managed to sneak out a few times at night by piling my pillows to make it look like me under the blankets. That was so lame, but it worked.

I still puked up first thing in the morning for about another month. Then it just stopped pretty much. Except I couldn't stand the smell of fried eggs. If I smelled a fried egg, everything came up, it didn't matter what time of day it was. At least I didn't get any weird cravings, except for grape Popsicles. I wanted those all the time.

When I told Justin that my dad wanted our baby to be adopted, he said that's what his parents said too. We were in the truck in the woods just off the dump road—the same place the condom had broken. "You wanna be stuck with a baby at your age?" He shook his head. "It's the best thing, Evie," he said. "The baby will get a good home and then it'll be like this didn't even happen."

Except it didn't work out that way.

Chapter Nine

I looked over at Justin, driving with one hand, elbow up on the doorframe. Since I'd had the baby I hadn't seen that much of him. I'd heard a rumor that he was seeing some other girl. Some of my so-called friends just couldn't wait to tell me stories like that. I didn't even listen because I knew it was just certain people who were jealous of me and Justin and wanted to hurt me. I'd even told Justin about all the gossip and he'd said it wasn't true—which I knew. He'd said he hadn't been around much because he didn't want to do anything to get my dad pissed off at me. But now we were going to be a family. Once we got to Montreal it'd just be me and Justin and Brianna and we'd be happy.

Justin looked down at the dashboard and muttered something I didn't hear. "What is it?" I asked.

"You got much money?" he said.

"Some," I answered carefully. "Why?" Brianna coughed in her sleep and moved around in the car seat. Her nose was running again. I found a Kleenex to wipe it. There was still some dried crusty stuff on one side, but I was afraid I'd wake her up if I tried to pick it off.

"We need to stop for gas."

"What do you mean?"

Justin leaned over and knocked on my head with his fist. "Knock, knock, Evie. Anyone home?"

I pulled my head away. "Cut it out, Justin," I said. "Do we have to stop now? Can't we go a little farther?"

"No."

I could tell by his voice that he was getting mad.

"You wanna get to Montreal?" he snapped. "You wanna get five more freakin' minutes down the road? We need gas."

"Okay. Fine," I said. I found my purse and pulled out a twenty. "Is this enough?" I asked, holding out the money.

"It's not going to get us very far," Justin said.

I found another twenty-dollar bill. "Here. But that's it. Brianna's gonna need diapers and food and stuff when we get to Montreal."

Justin mumbled something, then grabbed the money, jamming the bills into the pocket of his jeans. "Watch for a gas station," he said.

We both spotted the place at the same time—a convenience store with a couple of gas pumps. Just as Justin slowed down to turn, I smelled it. Something awful, a smell like a backed-up sewer, filled the truck.

"Aw, shit," Justin said. "What the—" He put the back of his hand up to his nose.

I remembered that smell from babysitting. It was the part I always hated. But this was different because Brianna was my baby. "It's just a dirty diaper," I said to Justin. "I can change her right here while you get the gas."

He pulled in next to the gas pumps, shut off the truck and got out. Brianna was still sleeping. She was such a good baby.

I undid the belt and lifted her out of the seat. She was warm and she didn't smell very good, but I could've held on to her forever. She settled in on my shoulder. I brushed bits of her fuzzy hair off her forehead. She had such long eyelashes—just like Justin. And her fingernails, they were so tiny. I'd never seen fingernails so little. How the heck was I going to cut them?

Brianna had the same long fingers as my mother. Piano-player fingers. My mother could play the piano without even looking at music. She used to say the music was in her head. She tried to teach me to play, but there wasn't any music in my head at all. And my fingers were short and stubby.

After my mom died, my dad sold the piano and gave all her CDs to the Sally Ann. He didn't even ask me if I wanted them.

I leaned over and kissed Brianna's fingers. Maybe there'd be music in her head. Maybe she'd play the piano for me when she was older, just the way my mother had done. All of a sudden there was a lump in my throat and I had to swallow hard a couple of times to get it to go down.

Chapter Ten

Brianna coughed, opened her eyes and made whimpering noises. "Shush, Mama's here," I told her.

She twisted in my arms and made more fussy sounds. It was hard to hold on to her and get out the diapers and stuff I needed, but I managed to get everything, spread the changing pad on the seat and lay her down. I had to open the truck door, stand outside and lean over the seat.

Brianna wouldn't stay still. She kicked and squirmed and I could barely get the snaps undone on her sleepers. She'd loaded her diaper. I didn't know what the Hansens had been feeding her, but it was rank. The smell made me gag. For a second I thought I was going to puke. I knew Justin would freak if I puked in his truck.

I turned my head and sucked in fresh air. Well, not totally fresh. It smelled kind of like gas a bit, but it was better than the baby poop smell.

I got the diaper off and folded it into a little package, but I didn't know what to do with it. I should've brought some garbage bags. I felt around under the seats and found a rag Justin used to rub spots off the truck. It wasn't exactly a rag. It felt kind of like a suede jacket.

I wiped all the poop off Brianna using a bunch of baby wipes. Then I wrapped them and the diaper up in Jason's truck-cleaning cloth. I hoped he wouldn't be mad, but there wasn't anything else to use.

Before I could get a new diaper on Brianna, she peed. Some of it ran off the changing pad onto the seat of the truck. I grabbed a handful of wipes and mopped up most of it. Finally I got the clean diaper on her and a new pair of sleepers. The diaper was a little bit big, but the sleepers fit perfectly.

Justin finally came back. He had a bag of Cheezies and a can of Coke in one hand. "It still stinks in here," he said.

"I need another bottle of water and some apple juice," I said as I fastened Brianna into the car seat again. He just stood there. "Justin." I glared at him.

He held out his hand. "I need more money." I gave him five dollars. He set his Coke and Cheezies on the seat. While he was gone I used another one of the baby wipes to get the crusty stuff off the baby's nose.

Justin came back with a bottle of water and a little bottle of juice. The water wasn't very cold.

"Didn't they have any water colder than this?" I said.

He shrugged. "That's all I saw."

I filled a baby bottle about half full of the apple juice. Brianna sucked it down. But before I could even undo the belt in the car seat, she puked. It went everywhere. On her clothes and blanket. In the car seat. On the truck seat.

"Aw, Jesus," Justin shouted. "There's freakin' barf all over my truck."

I'd already grabbed a handful of baby wipes from the box. I cleaned Brianna's face and hands first. "She's just a baby," I said over my shoulder to Justin. "She can't help it. Babies puke. And maybe you don't remember, but you've puked in this truck a couple of times."

"This is a total piss-up," Justin raved. "I just cleaned the entire inside last night. Now it stinks."

"Too friggin' bad," I yelled at Justin.

He grabbed the can of Coke and fired it across the service station lot. It hit a telephone pole and bounced on the pavement. Brown foam sprayed all over the ground.

I'd pretty much cleaned up Brianna, the car seat and the truck. I dumped a heap of dirty wipes in the garbage can between the gas pumps. I wadded up the blanket that was over the baby and threw that away too.

The cloth with the poopy diaper and wipes was still on the truck floor. I picked it up and turned to throw it away too.

"What the hell are you doing with that?" Justin yelled. "That's my polishing cloth. Don't throw that out."

I dropped everything in the garbage. "It's a rag," I said. "You can get another one. I needed something to wrap up the dirty diaper and stuff."

"That's not a rag. You are so stupid! That's a polishing cloth for doing the truck bumpers."

"Big hairy deal," I shouted back. "Like anyone cares what your stupid bumpers look like." I reached down to find a blanket in my backpack, and Justin grabbed my arm.

"I'm not doing this, Evie," he said. His face was so close to mine that bits of spit hit me as he said the words. "I'm done. We're going back."

"No." I tried to wrench my arm away but he held on tightly.

"Yes."

"You're Brianna's father and you don't even care about her."

"I don't want to be her father," Justin said. "She was a freakin' accident. We screwed around and we screwed up. She's only here 'cause the condom broke. I'm not her father, Evie, and you're not her mother. Not for real. Her real mother and father are back there in that house probably going crazy worrying about her."

I finally managed to twist out of his grasp. I could see the red imprint of his fingers on my wrist.

"We're her family," I said. "We're the only family she needs." Brianna was crying. I put my hand on her head. "You're scaring her, Justin."

"Give it up, Evie," Justin said. He pulled his hand through his hair again. "We're not a family. She has one but we're not it. You think you're gonna be a fashion designer in Montreal? Right. You'll end up working at the dollar store. You saw that house. Those people can give her stuff that you can't."

"You mean like a big house and fancy clothes? That stuff doesn't matter. Nobody can love Brianna like I do." I straightened her little hat and she twisted her head away from me.

"She doesn't even like you, Evie," Justin said quietly.

"She just doesn't remember me. But she will," I said. "She spent nine whole months inside me. She knows me. She'll remember."

"You just don't get it. It's not happening." Justin wiped his hand down the side of his face. "We'd be lucky to even get close to Montreal. You think the cops aren't going to catch up with us? You kidnapped a baby, Evie. She isn't yours anymore."

"You know, you're acting like you don't even love your own kid," I said.

"I don't," Justin said. "But the Hansens do. We have to take her back. Maybe they'll let you come and visit and stuff. You know, like at Christmas and her birthday."

"I don't want to visit a couple of times a year," I shouted. "I want to be with her all the time. And after this do you really think they'd let me anywhere near her? I'm not going back."

"I'm not doing this," Justin said. "It's over, Evie." He snapped the side of my head with his thumb and finger. "Get that through your head." Then he turned and stalked away.

My heart was pounding and my hands were shaking. I made myself take some deep breaths in and out, but they were all jerky. I got back into the truck and bent over Brianna. She'd stopped crying.

Her face was flushed. "Don't worry," I told her. "Nobody's taking you away from me. Not Justin. Not the police. Not anybody."

I looked around the service station lot. Then I saw Justin inside the building. He was talking on the phone.

No.

Chapter Eleven

It felt like someone had punched me in the gut. Tears filled my eyes and rolled down my face. I swiped them away with the edge of my hand. There was no time. "It'll be okay," I whispered to the baby.

I felt around on the floor of the truck and shoved everything into the backpack—the bottle of water, the rest of the juice, my purse, everything. Then I unfastened the seat belt that was holding the car seat in place. I looked over at the convenience store again. Justin was still on the phone. My heart felt like it had jumped up into my throat, but I knew what I had to do.

I reached up and turned off the little dome light in case Justin looked this way. I opened the truck door, slid down off the seat and hiked my pack onto my back. Then I grabbed the car seat and, staying low to the ground, scurried across the parking lot and let the darkness swallow us.

There wasn't any traffic on the road, but I stayed way over on the edge of the pavement just in case. It was slow walking with the car seat. It kept banging against my leg every time I took a step. After a few minutes of walking, I looked down the embankment next to the road. I could just barely make out some kind of gravel trail that wound away through the bushes. If I could get down there, I thought, there was no way Justin would be able to find me.

The bank wasn't that steep—mostly big rocks and grass. "Okay, okay, we can do this," I said to Brianna. I wrapped both arms around the car seat and eased my way down, feeling with my feet because I couldn't really see where we were going. One foot slipped on the long grass and I lost my balance and ended up sliding the rest of the way on my butt, but I held on tight to Brianna. I set the car seat down on the ground and leaned in to check on her.

She gave me a wide-eyed *what-the-hell-was-that?* look. "We're okay. We made it," I told her. Her nose was drippy again. I found a Kleenex in my pocket and wiped it one more time. I wished babies knew how to blow.

I got up and brushed the dirt off my pants. We were right by the edge of the trail. It turned up ahead so I couldn't see where it went, but I knew it had to be a lot safer than being up on the road. I shifted my backpack to one side a little and picked up the car seat. I suddenly remembered something my mother used to say whenever we were going somewhere—even just to the store. She'd grin at me like it was some kind of big adventure and then she'd say, "We're off to see the wizard." I never even knew what that meant. But I smiled at Brianna and said it anyway, "We're off to see the wizard."

I followed the trail because I didn't really know what else to do. I needed to find a bus station so I could get to Montreal...or anywhere, as long as it was away from here. I finally figured out how to hold the car seat on one side so it didn't keep hitting my leg, but it was heavy and I still had to keep shifting it from one arm to the other.

When the trail came out of the trees I could see another road running beside it, but there were enough bushes and we were far enough away that I figured no one would spot us. And the trail seemed to be getting closer to some kind of downtown. If I could find a place with a phone, I could look in the phone book for a bus station.

My feet hurt and my arms ached, but every time I thought about stopping I remembered Justin on that phone, selling me out. That made me feel like there was a hand inside me, squeezing my stomach, and I'd walk faster then because I knew I had to get away from Justin, from this place, from everyone, because nobody was going to take my baby away from me.

Finally the trail took us by a park and a big building that reminded me of the Y at home. There were a couple of benches out in front of the place, and I sat down for a rest. The bottoms of my feet were burning.

I set Brianna up beside me. She was asleep again. I studied her face, trying to figure out who she looked like—Justin or me. She had my hair, that's for sure. And she yelled like me when she was pissed. But I couldn't tell about the rest. Mostly she just looked like herself.

Everyone always said I looked like my mom except for I had my dad's temper. I didn't see how I looked like her at all, except for the color of our hair—a sort of dark reddish brown. I mean, I wouldn't have minded looking like her because she was beautiful. She had brown eyes like chocolate, and her skin was so perfect she didn't have to put anything on it. And she could eat anything and not gain weight.

But the best thing about her was her laugh. It would make you laugh too when you didn't even know what was funny. I missed my mom laughing. Nobody laughed in my house after she died. My dad hardly even smiled.

Three girls came across the grass in my direction. They were talking so they didn't even notice me until they were almost at the bench, but then one of them spotted Brianna.

"Oh, look, a baby," she squealed. She bent over the car seat. "She's so cute."

"Thanks," I said.

The other two leaned in for a look. "She's so tiny," one of them said.

"Is she yours?" the first girl asked me.

I nodded.

"She's adorable. How old is she?"

"Five months," I said. I reached over and pushed Brianna's hat back a bit so they could see her face.

"Look at her chubby little cheeks," one of them said.

"I'm Stephanie," the first girl said. She was wearing a purple sparkly top and jeans, and her blond hair was in a high ponytail with long bits down around her face. "I don't think I've seen you before. You must go to Cumberland."

"Yeah," I said. "I'm E—" Wait a minute. I shouldn't use my real name. "—Eden. My name's Eden," I said.

"What's your baby's name?" Stephanie asked.

"Brianna," I said.

One of Stephanie's friends looked up from the car seat. "I like that name," she said. "It's classy."

"Are you going to the dance?" the other girl asked. Her dark hair was all curls, just the way I wished I could get my hair to look, but it never did, even with a perm.

"No. I'm...um...I'm waiting for my boyfriend."

Stephanie looked at her watch. "Hey, we better get going," she said. She gave me a little wave. "See you, Eden."

"Yeah, see you," I said. I watched them cut across the grass and go into the building. I heard a burst of music, for a second, when the door opened. I wondered what Jade and my other friends were doing at home. They would have already gone swimming and hooked up with some guys. They were probably at a party somewhere now.

I looked over at Brianna. I didn't care about parties and dances anymore. I was a mother now and I had a lot more important stuff to do.

Chapter Twelve

My stomach growled. I realized how hungry I was. It had been hours since I'd eaten. I'd had lunch. Had I had any supper? I couldn't remember. I stood up, put on my pack and picked up Brianna. There had to be somewhere around here where I could get something to eat.

I headed back along the trail again. I heard a barking dog and a car door slam, but I didn't see any other people. Did this whole place shut down once it got dark? I was watching for a Dairy Queen or something like that, but all I passed was houses. How rinky-dink was this place if it didn't have a Dairy Queen or a Burger Barn?

And then finally I saw something. The sign on the roof said *Fern's*, and it was almost as big as the building. There weren't any cars out front, but there was a lit red *Open* sign in the window. My stomach growled again. Okay, so it wasn't the Burger Barn, but it would do. I left the trail and started across the road.

Fern's smelled like coffee and burgers inside. Not a bad smell at all. There was a counter at the far end and a bunch of shiny stools with red vinyl seats. There were booths down the two long walls and tables in the middle of the room. I slid into one of the booths on the window side and set Brianna beside me in her seat. The high, dark-wood backs reminded me of church pews. I could watch the road, and the bathrooms were just behind me in case we had to get out of sight fast.

There was a woman behind the counter. She came around it and walked over to me. She was wearing jeans and a green apron. "Hi," she said. "What can I get you?" Brianna was awake and making fussy noises. "Hi, cutie-pie," the waitress said to her.

"Um, could I have a cheeseburger with fries and a large milk?" I said.

"Sure." She didn't write my order down, but then it wasn't like there was a lot to remember. She smiled at Brianna. "I can warm up a bottle if you'd like," she said.

"It's okay," I said. "I have stuff for her."

The waitress gave me the smile this time. "I thought you probably did," she said. "If you want to give me a bottle, I can stick it in some hot water for you to warm it up. It's a lot easier than holding it under the tap in the bathroom." She jerked her head in the direction of the washrooms. "Water doesn't get that hot in there anyway."

I couldn't remember anything from that book I got at the library about warming up bottles. But then I hadn't really read the whole thing. There were about three hundred pages, and I hadn't had a lot of time.

"She's not that crazy about the formula," I said. "I don't know if she'll like it if it's hot."

The waitress gave me a funny look. She looked from me to Brianna and back again. "Not hot," she said. "Just warm. Babies, little ones anyway, like their bottles warmed up a bit." She frowned. "She is yours, isn't she?"

I put one hand on the car seat. "I'm her mother," I said, "but someone else has been looking after her for me. Just for a while."

I found a bottle of formula in my bag and held it out. "Maybe you could warm it up. Please. If it's not too much trouble."

She smiled again and took the bottle. "Sure, no problem."

I leaned over and looked out the window. A car went by, and a minivan, but I didn't see any sign of Justin's truck or the police. I slumped against the back of the booth. How could Justin do this? I thought we were in love. We were in love. We'd made Brianna.

There was a sour taste all of a sudden at the back of my throat, and my eyes felt prickly, like I might cry. I closed them for a second. I couldn't think about Justin. As soon as I had something to eat I was going to have to figure out how to get me and Brianna to Montreal.

And then it hit me. I couldn't take Brianna to Montreal. Justin would've told them that was where I was going. They'd probably have police waiting at the bus station in Montreal. I pressed my hand over my mouth. Okay, okay, so I'd go in the other direction. I could go to Halifax. Then in a few days or maybe a week, when they weren't looking for me there anymore, I'd go to Montreal.

I looked over at Brianna. She was chewing her fist. Her hat had slid way down to her eyebrows. I reached over and pulled it off. Her dark hair was matted against her head. I tried to fluff it up a bit, but it was all sweaty and stuck down. "Even on a bad hair day, you're beautiful," I told her.

There was more green gunk on her nose. I had to dig all the way to the bottom of my backpack to find a clean Kleenex. I wiped her nose and she made a crabby face at me and then sneezed.

"Bless you," the waitress said. She handed me the bottle. "It should be okay," she said. "I checked it." She shrugged. "I have two of my own."

"Thank you," I said.

Brianna gave the bottle a suspicious look. She pressed her lips together like she had before. Then she yawned and I popped the nipple in her mouth. She sucked on it, and this time she didn't spit it out. I'd have to remember to warm up the bottle from now on.

"You want onions on your cheese-burger?" the waitress called from behind the counter.

"Please," I said.

"And gravy on the fries?"

My mouth was starting to water. "Yes, please. Lots."

Brianna sucked hungrily at her bottle. About a quarter of it was already gone when the waitress brought my food. I was starving. I took both of the baby's hands and put them around the bottle so she could hold it and my own hands would be free to eat. But when I let go, the bottle fell into the car seat. Brianna let out a yowl.

I stuck the bottle back in her mouth, held on to it with one hand and tried to use my fork with the other, but it was the wrong hand and I couldn't even spear one French fry. I set the fork down and tried to put Brianna's hands around the bottle again, but she didn't seem to get what I wanted her to do.

The waitress was two tables over, putting napkins in a dispenser. "I think she's a bit too young yet to hold on to a bottle," she said. "Would you like me to feed her?" She gestured to the empty room. "I don't mind. It's not exactly busy tonight."

My stomach growled again. "Um, okay. Thanks," I said. I pulled the car seat over a little.

The waitress came and sat down. She took the bottle from me. "I'm Leslie, by the way," she said.

What name had I given those girls? Oh yeah. "I'm Eden," I said. "And this is Brianna."

There was real cheese on the burger, not the kind that came all wrapped up in plastic. And the fries were homemade. For a couple of minutes I ate without talking. A bit of milk dribbled down the side of Brianna's chin. Leslie wiped it up with a paper napkin.

"How old is Brianna?" she asked.

"Five months," I said.

Leslie studied the baby's face, then looked at me. My heart started to race. Had she figured something out?

"She has your eyes," she said at last.

It was all right. I felt my legs go wobbly. It was a good thing I wasn't standing up. I popped another French fry in my mouth. They were so good. "How old are your kids?" I asked.

"Kyra is eight and Sam, my little guy, is six." She shook her head. "It feels like it was just yesterday that they were this small." She ran a finger over Brianna's hand. "Look at those fingers. She'll be playing piano someday."

"My mom played," I said.

"What about you?" Leslie asked.

I laughed. "No. I can't play anything and I can't sing. But I can draw. My art teacher says I'm really creative. I'm going to be a fashion designer." I almost said, "in Montreal," but then I caught myself.

"So, you make your own clothes?"

I shook my head. "No. I can't sew or anything like that. But I'm really good at putting a look together—like a shirt and pants with the right shoes and stuff. I dress my friends all the time and go shopping and help them figure out what to buy."

"Maybe you should work in a clothing store," Leslie said. "Whenever I go shopping I can never find anyone to help me decide what goes together."

"You can make a lot more money as a fashion designer," I said.

Leslie took a Kleenex out of her apron pocket and wiped Brianna's nose. That reminded me that I needed to get some stuff, like more Kleenex, before we got on a bus. "When I was your age I wanted to be a singer," Leslie said.

I looked at her. Her blond hair was done back in a long braid, and she didn't have any wrinkles. "You still could be," I said. "You're not that old."

Leslie laughed. "Thanks, but that kind of life—up all night and being on the road—doesn't work when you have two kids and no husband."

"But there's day care."

"Good day care costs money. And it's pretty hard to find one that's open till two in the morning when the clubs close."

"I never thought of that," I said, taking the last bite of my burger. "But it doesn't seem fair that you have to work here when you really want to be a singer."

"This is not a bad job," Leslie said. "I get to cook, which I like. And the woman who owns the place, she's really good about letting me change shifts if one of my kids gets sick or something." Brianna finished the bottle and Leslie set it on the table. "As long as my kids are okay, I'm happy, you know?"

I nodded. I did know. Brianna being happy was why I'd done this. I just wished I could have made Justin understand that.

Chapter Thirteen

I wiped my hands on a napkin and took Brianna out of the car seat. She wiggled and fussed as I lifted her onto my shoulder to burp her. "Please burp," I said to her, gently patting her back. She sneezed on my neck instead.

"Bless you," Leslie said.

Brianna seemed warm in my arms and I realized she needed a clean diaper. She was kicking my ribs with her foot.

"Have you ever tried laying her across your lap to burp her?" Leslie asked.

"Umm, what do you mean?" I said.

"Can I take her?"

I hesitated for a second, then handed Brianna over.

Leslie held her up for a second. "Hello there, cutie-bug," she said. "Where are all your burps?" She laid Brianna face down across her lap with the baby's head in the crook of her arm and her hand at Brianna's waist. Then she rubbed slow circles in the middle of Brianna's back. "Like this," Leslie said. "Don't press too hard." And then Brianna burped, a loud one, just like Justin.

"I bet that feels better," Leslie said with a grin. She sat the baby up on her lap. I noticed Brianna didn't squirm or try to get away. She couldn't like Leslie more than me. I was her mother.

I reached over for Brianna. "I have to change her," I said.

"They've got a changing table in the ladies' room," Leslie said, getting to her feet. I slid out of the booth, pulling the backpack behind me. "You want any dessert?" she asked as she gathered my dishes. "We have apple pie, blueberry, lemon meringue and banana cream."

"Um, yeah, banana cream, please," I said. "I'll be right back."

I took Brianna into the bathroom. At first I couldn't find the changing table. Then I realized it wasn't a table. It was just a thing that folded down from the wall, and I knew I couldn't change Brianna on that. There was no way I could keep her from falling off and get a diaper on her at the same time.

So I put the changing pad I'd used in the truck down on the bathroom floor. It looked pretty clean—in fact the whole bathroom kind of smelled like Javex. I figured Brianna would be a lot safer on the floor.

This diaper was a lot easier to change than the poopy one was. And I was getting better at the snaps on the sleepers. I washed my hands and then

I picked up Brianna and my stuff and headed back out to the table.

I could hear voices as I came out the bathroom door. Leslie was talking to somebody. I looked over toward the counter and saw a police officer standing there with his back to me.

Chapter Fourteen

I couldn't breathe, and my feet seemed to be stuck to the ground. The police officer turned around and there was nowhere to run. I held Brianna tight against me, one arm around her body and one across her shoulders. I wasn't letting go.

"Thanks," he said to Leslie. "See ya."

He walked toward me, and I saw he was carrying a big brown paper bag with a piece of paper stapled at the top. He smiled as he passed me. I don't know if I smiled back or not. Then he was out the door.

I sagged against the wall. My legs were all shaky, as if I'd forgotten how to walk, but somehow I stumbled back to the table. Through the window I saw the red lights of the police car disappear down the street. I took a deep breath and let it go. We were safe, and pretty soon we'd be on a bus going far away from here, and no one would be able to take my baby away from me.

Leslie came over with my pie as I was putting Brianna into the car seat. The baby's nose was red and sore-looking from being wiped so much. "Is there a store that's open anywhere around here?" I asked. "I need to get some cold medicine."

Leslie frowned. "You know you can't give that to a baby, right?" She bent over and felt the baby's cheeks and forehead. "She is warm. I think she probably has a fever."

"Are you sure I can't just give her some of that stuff they advertise on TV?" I asked. "You know that commercial with that guy from the show about all the doctors. He's the tall one with the blue eyes. I wouldn't give her very much."

"You can't give her anything like that. She's a baby. She's just a few months old. But you could take her to the after-hours clinic and get one of the nurses to take a look at her."

I felt Brianna's face. She was really warm. I must have looked worried because Leslie said, "I'm sure she's all right. Babies get fevers all the time. The clinic is just down the street." She leaned across the table and pointed out the window. "See those lights just down there? That's it. They're open till midnight."

I could feel that lump again in my throat. I couldn't finish my pie because I couldn't swallow anything past it. Brianna was whining and coughing, and there was gunk on her nose again. But how could I take her to the clinic? They'd ask too many questions. She grabbed my finger, tightly, the way she did before. All I could think was *I'll die. I'll die if they take her away from me. I can't give her back.*

My heart was pounding so loudly I was surprised Leslie didn't hear it. She was gathering the salt and pepper shakers from the tables and setting them on the counter.

I looked at Brianna. Maybe she wasn't that sick. Okay, so she was coughing and her nose was running, but that was just a cold. A cold wasn't that big a deal. And even Leslie had said that babies get fevers all the time. As soon as we got to Halifax I'd take her to a doctor. First thing. But right now we had to get going.

"Excuse me. Can you tell me where the bus station is?" I asked Leslie. She was filling the salt shakers from a giant box of salt.

"Sure," she said. "Go left when you go out the door and then left again at the corner. You can't miss it." She paused. "And the clinic is just up to the right across the street. Like I said, you can see the lights from here."

"Thank you," I said. I gave her a twenty and waited for my change. Then I put on my jacket, gathered all my stuff and tucked the blanket around Brianna.

"Bye," Leslie said. "Take good care of that little one."

"I will," I said. "Bye." By the time the police showed up to ask questions, if they even did, Brianna and I would be long gone.

Chapter Fifteen

Brianna started coughing again as soon as we were outside in the cold air. I set the car seat down and lifted her out. For once she didn't kick or squirm. She just settled in close to me with her head on my shoulder. "Just a couple more hours and we'll be safe," I whispered. "I promise as soon as we get to Halifax we'll find a doctor."

I could hear Brianna's wheezy breathing and it made me think about my mother. I don't know how old I was, six maybe, and I was sick. It was more than just a cold. I remember she rubbed some kind of awful-smelling stuff on my chest, and she sat by my bed all night. Every time I woke up she was there with a glass of water and a cool cloth for my head.

I felt a sharp pain stab my chest. Missing my mother hurt the same as thinking about giving up Brianna. Tears filled my eyes and I had to blink hard to make them go away. I didn't have any time to cry. I hooked the handle of the baby seat over my arm. Left, she'd said, and then left around the corner. I walked down the street with the car seat bumping against my hip.

I turned the corner. There were two big buses pulled up in front of the bus station.

And two big police officers at the door.

I backed up, turned around and started walking fast up the street. Goddamn Justin. I had to stop for a second so I could catch my breath. I pressed my cheek against Brianna's. "It's okay," I said. "It's okay." I didn't need Justin. I could do this without him.

There was an alley next to the diner, narrow and dark, with a big Dumpster against the wall about halfway down. The Dumpster stank, but not that much, and I'd smelled worse. There were a couple of wooden things stacked against the wall by the Dumpster. They looked like low wooden platforms. I give them a push with my foot, but they didn't even wobble and they were better than sitting on the ground. I set the car seat down and shifted Brianna from one shoulder to the other. I didn't have anything to wipe her nose with, so I used the edge of my sleeve.

I couldn't believe Justin had ratted me out, but he had, and if I thought about it I was going to be so mad or even cry, and I didn't have time for that. A couple of tears came from somewhere and slipped down my cheek.

I rubbed them away with the back of my hand and swallowed the fear creeping up from my stomach.

Okay, so we couldn't take a bus. We could hitch. I'd walk back up to the highway and we'd find a ride—anywhere, just away from here. Off in the distance I heard a police siren. Were they looking for me? I listened. No, it was going away from here.

Brianna couldn't seem to stop coughing. "It'll be okay," I told her, tucking the blanket closer around her. "Don't be scared. They're not going to take you away from me." I was shaking. Not because I was scared. It was just cold in between the Dumpster and the building.

I stood up and the baby puked. All over my sweater, down my back, even in my hair there was baby puke. My stomach flip-flopped, and for a second I was afraid I was going to heave too. I closed my eyes for a moment and started breathing through my mouth. Brianna was crying and, I couldn't help it, so was I.

I cleaned her up with the blanket and a handful of baby wipes. Then I put her in the car seat.

There was barf all over my jacket. And there were only a couple of wipes left in the package. I got the puke out of my hair, but I couldn't clean it off my jacket. I was just going to have to go without it. We'd just walk fast, out to the highway. I could do this.

I bent down and picked up Brianna again. I stood there, rocking back and forth, and she stopped crying. She smelled like barf, and I could hear every breath she took. And with our faces together I could feel how warm she was.

My tears fell on her cheek. I wiped them away but they kept on coming. I could hear the sirens again. I wanted my own mother. She would know what to do. But the only mother was me.

I rocked Brianna, back and forth, until she fell asleep in my arms. The only sound was her breathing. I kissed her, her forehead, her cheek, the top of her head. She was my baby. "Nobody loves you like I do," I whispered. My hands were shaking. Every part of me was shaking. "I'm your real mother," I told her.

I hooked the backpack over one shoulder and walked down the alley. There were no people around, but I could hear the traffic in the distance out on the highway.

I didn't even stop walking. I was the only mother there was. I crossed the street and turned right. Down toward the lights of the clinic.

Darlene Ryan is the author of *Rules for Life*, an ALA Best Book nominee. Darlene lives in Fredericton, New Brunswick.

Visit her website at www.darleneryan.com

Other titles in the
Orca Soundings series

Other titles in the Orca Soundings series

Visit www.orcabook.com for more information.

More Orca Soundings

Crush
by Carrie Mac

Isn't she fazed by any of this? Does she do this all the time? Make unsuspecting, seemingly straight girls squirm? Or am I making it all up? But making up what? The butterflies are real. The fact that I want to kiss her is real.

Would kissing a girl be different from kissing boys? If all I did was kiss her, would that make me queer? Are you queer just for thinking it? Or does doing it make you queer? And what if I don't want to be queer? Do I get a say in this at all?

Because of a moment of indiscretion, Hope's parents send her to New York to spend the summer with her sister. Miserable, Hope ends up meeting Nat and developing a powerful crush. The only problem is that Nat is a girl. Hope is pretty sure she isn't gay. Or is she? Struggling with new feelings, fitting in and a strange city far from home, Hope finds that love—and acceptance—comes in many different forms.

More Orca Soundings

Stuffed
by Eric Walters

"So, do we have a deal?" Mr. Evans asked.

"Unbelievable," I muttered under my breath.

"I don't understand," Mr. Evans said.

"The whole thing is unbelievable. First you try to threaten me. Then you try to bribe me. And now you do the two together, trying to bribe me and threatening me if I don't take the bribe."

"I don't like to think of it in those terms," he said.

When Ian and his classmates watch a documentary about the health concerns of eating fast food, Ian decides to start a boycott against a multinational food chain. Can Ian stand up for what he believes in? Can he take on a corporate behemoth and win?

More Orca Soundings

Exposure
by Patricia Murdoch

I was happier than I had been for a long time. Everything was crashing down around Dana. Finally I was getting some justice. But I wanted a bigger helping. This wasn't enough. I had to do something.

I went into the washroom and dug a marker out of my pencil case. I drew a box and a couple of circles, with lines for a flash going off, on the outer wall of the first cubicle. No one would be able to miss it. It didn't look exactly like a camera, but it would do. And for the finishing touch I wrote SMILE DANA, with a happy face right beside it.

Exit Point
by Laura Langston

"I'm not dead. I'm still me. I still have a body and everything."

"You are still you, but you don't have a body. What you're seeing is a thought form." He points to a tall gold urn up by the minister. *"Your body is in there. You were cremated."*

Thunk thunk, thunk thunk. My heart pounds in my chest. Dread mushrooms in my stomach. Sweat beads on my forehead. *"But everybody knows death is the end. That there's nothing left but matter."*

"Death is only the beginning, Logan. Hannah knows that. Lots of people do."

Logan always takes the easy way out. After a night of drinking and driving, he wakes up to find he has been involved in a car accident and is dead. With the help of his guide, Wade, and the spirit of his grandmother, he realizes he has taken the wrong exit. He wasn't meant to die. His life had a purpose—to save his sister!